TRUCKS LINE UP

BY JON SCIESZKA

CHARACTERS AND ENVIRONMENTS DEVELOPED BY THE

DAVID SHANNON   LOREN LONG   DAVID GORDON

ILLUSTRATION CREW:

Executive Producer:

INDUSTRIES

Creative Supervisor: Nina Rappaport Brown ○ Drawings by: Dan Root ○ Color by: Antonio Reyna

Art Director: Aviva Shur

READY-TO-ROLL

SIMON SPO

NEW YORK   LONDON

Cuyahoga Falls
Library
Cuyahoga Falls, Ohio

SIMON SPOTLIGHT

An imprint of Simon & Schuster Children's Publishing Division
1230 Avenue of the Americas, New York, NY 10020

Copyright © 2011 by JRS Worldwide, LLC. TRUCKTOWN AND JON SCIESZKA'S
TRUCKTOWN and design are trademarks of JRS Worldwide, LLC. All rights reserved,
including the right of reproduction in whole or in part in any form. SIMON SPOTLIGHT,
READY-TO-READ, and colophon are registered trademarks of Simon & Schuster, Inc.

For information about special discounts for bulk purchases, please contact Simon & Schuster Special Sales at 1-866-506-1949
or business@simonandschuster.com. Manufactured in the United States of America 0111 LAK
First Simon Spotlight edition February 2011 10 9 8 7 6 5 4 3 2 1
Library of Congress Cataloging-in-Publication Data
Scieszka, Jon.
Trucks line up / by Jon Scieszka ; artwork created by the Design Garage: David Gordon, Loren Long, David Shannon. — 1st Simon
Spotlight ed.
p. cm. — (Ready-to-read) (Jon Scieszka's Trucktown)
Summary: As soon as Jack Truck wakes up he gets the other trucks in line, but somehow he misses Pete.
[1. Trucks—Fiction] I. Design Garage. II. Title.
PZ7.S41267Tnt 2011
[E]—dc22
2009035952
ISBN 978-1-4169-4147-7 (pbk)
ISBN 978-1-4169-4158-3 (hc)

Jack wakes up.
He gives his call:
"Trucks **line up!**"

"Blue trucks here.
Red trucks there.

Trucks line **up!"**

"Trucks in pink.
Trucks in green.
Big Rig—any time you want.

Trucks line up!"

"That should do it.
Here we go."

"Hey," says Pete. "What about me?"

"Ooops. Sorry, Pete.
Red? Blue?
Scraper? Flasher?"

"No,
no, no,
and
no."

"Um . . .
Orange with scooper,
ladder, muffler,
and a name that starts
with P?"

"Yes!" says Pete.

"Now we are ready.
Every truck.

Ready. Set. Go!"

Trucks go left.

Trucks go right.

Trucks go down.

Trucks go up.

Trucks go round and
round and round.

Then Jack honks
his horn and
gives his call:

"TRUCKS . . .

LINE . . .

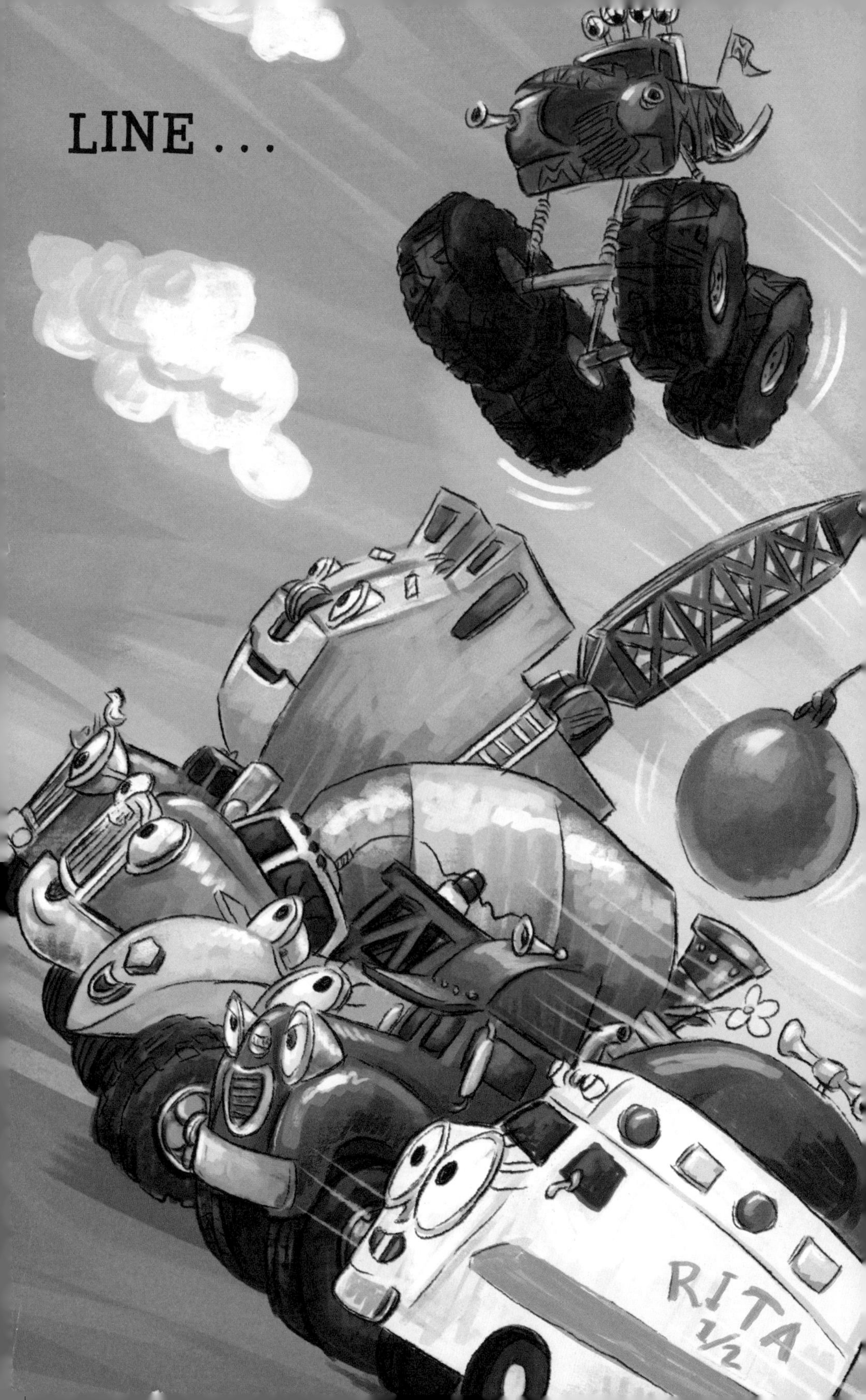

. . . UP!"